First published in hardback in Great Britain by
HarperCollins Publishers Ltd in 1992
10 9 8 7 6 5 4 3
First published in Great Britain in Picture Lions in 1994
10 9 8 7 6 5 4 3 2 1
Picture Lions is an imprint of the Children's Division,
part of HarperCollins Publishers Limited,
77-85 Fulham Palace Road, Hammersmith,
London W6 8JB
ISBN: 0 00 193662-X (Hardback)
ISBN: 0 00 664136-9 (Picture Lions)
The author and illustrator assert the moral right to be
identified as the author and illustrator of the work.
Text © Michael Bond 1972
Illustrations © HarperCollins Publishers Ltd 1992
A CIP catalogue record for this title is
available from the British Library.
Produced by HarperCollins Hong Kong

Paddington's Garden

Michael Bond

PictureLions
An Imprint of HarperCollins*Publishers*

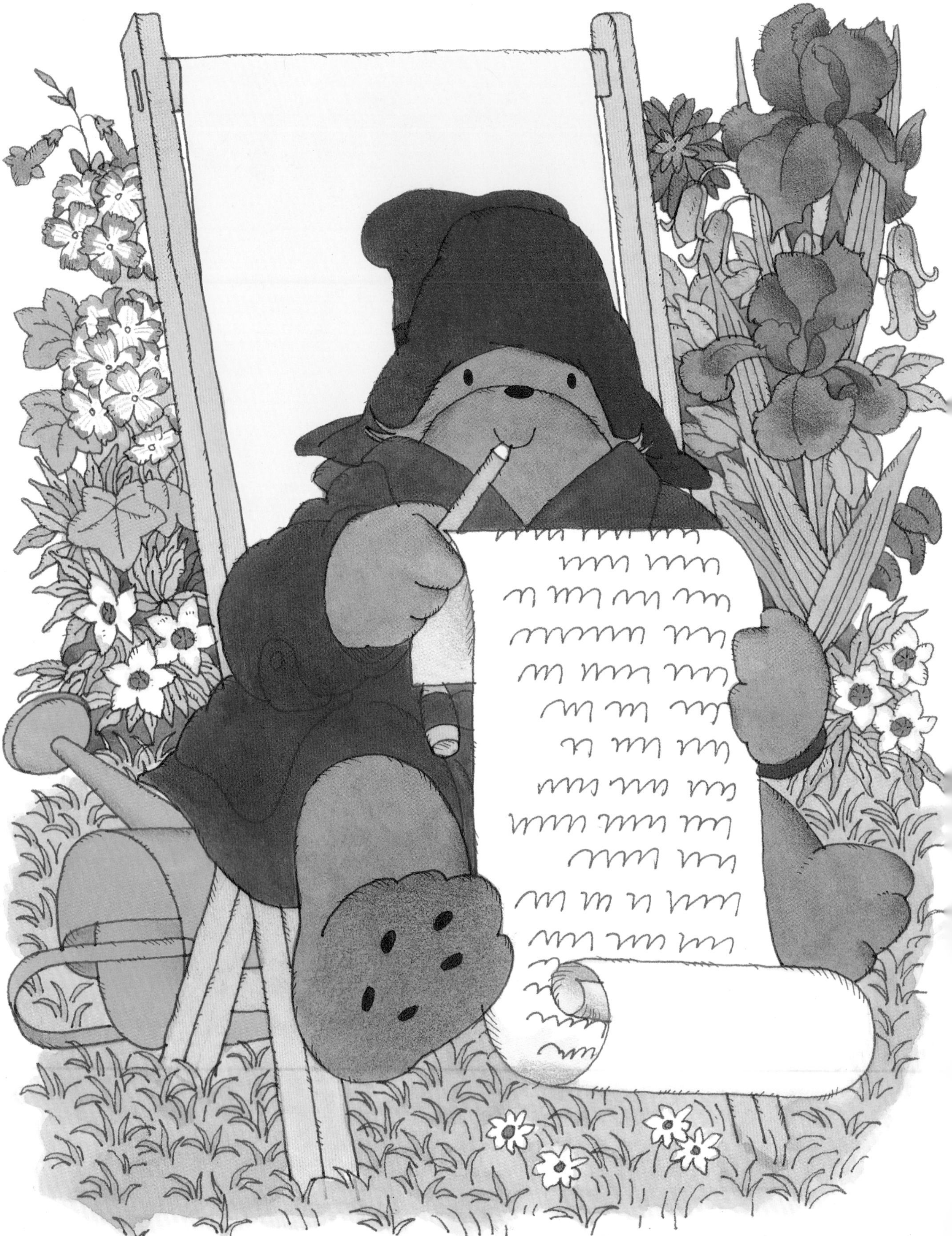

One day Paddington decided to make a list of all the nice things there were about being a bear and living with the Browns at number thirty-two Windsor Gardens.

It was a long list and he had almost reached the end of the paper when he suddenly realised he'd left out one of the nicest things of all... the garden itself!

Paddington liked the Browns' garden. It was quiet and peaceful, and there were times when it might not have been in London at all.

But nice gardens usually mean a lot of hard work, and after a day at his office Mr Brown often wished it wasn't quite so large.

It was Mrs Brown who first thought of giving Jonathan, Judy and Paddington a piece each of their own.

"It will keep them out of mischief," she said.

"And it will help you at the same time."

So Mr Brown marked out three squares, and to make it more exciting he said he would give a prize to whoever had the best idea.

Early next morning all three set to work.

Judy thought she would grow some flowers, and Jonathan started to make a paved garden, but Paddington didn't know what to do.

Gardening was much harder than it looked – especially with paws, and he soon grew tired of digging.

In the end he decided to do some shopping.

    He had some savings left over from his pocket money and he bought a wheelbarrow, a trug, a trowel, and a large packet of assorted seeds.

    It seemed very good value indeed – especially as he still had two pence left over.

The shopkeeper told him that when planning a new garden it was a good idea to stand some way away first, in order to picture what it would look like when it was finished. So, taking a jar of his best chunky marmalade, Paddington set out to visit the nearby building site.

By the time he got there it was the middle of the morning, and as the men were all at their tea break he sat down on a pile of bricks, put the jar of marmalade on a wooden platform for safety, and then peered hopefully towards the Browns' garden.

After sitting there for some while without getting a single idea Paddington decided to try taking a short walk instead.

When he got back his eyes nearly popped out.

A man was emptying the concrete mixer on the very spot where he'd left his jar of chunky marmalade.

At that moment the foreman came round the corner and seeing the look on Paddington's face he stopped to ask what was wrong.

Paddington pointed to the pile of wet cement.

"All my chunks have been buried!" he exclaimed hotly.

The foreman called his men together. "There's a
young bear gentleman here who's lost some very
valuable chunks," he said urgently.

They set to work clearing the cement.
    Soon the ground was covered with small piles,
but still there was no sign of Paddington's jar.

Suddenly there was a whirring sound from somewhere overhead and to Paddington's surprise a platform landed at his feet.

"My marmalade!" he exclaimed thankfully.

"Your marmalade?" echoed the foreman, staring at the jar. "Did you say marmalade?"

"That's right," said Paddington. "I put it there ready for my elevenses. It must have been taken up by mistake."

It was the foreman's turn to look as if he could hardly believe his eyes.

"That's special quick-drying cement!" he wailed. "It's probably going rock-hard already—ruined by a

bear's marmalade! No one will give me two pence for it now!"

Paddington opened his suitcase and felt in the secret compartment. "I will," he said eagerly.

Paddington took the lumps of concrete home in his
wheelbarrow and worked hard in his garden for the
rest of the day. When the builders saw the rockery
he had made with the concrete they were most
impressed and gave Paddington several plants to
finish it off for the time being...

...until his seeds started to grow.

Paddington's rockery fitted in so well with
Jonathan's paved garden and Judy's flower bed it
looked as though the whole thing had been planned.

Mr Brown was so pleased he decided to give them
all an extra week's pocket money, and that afternoon
they celebrated by having tea in the new garden.

After it was over Paddington stayed on for a
while in order to finish off his list of all the nice
things there were about being a bear and living at
number thirty-two Windsor Gardens.

He had one more important item to add.

MY ROCKERY

Then he signed his name and added his special
paw print...

...just to show it was genuine.